A NOTE TO PARENTS

Reading Aloud with Your Child

Research shows that reading books aloud is the single most valuable support parents can provide in helping children learn to read.

- Be a ham! The more enthusiasm you display, the more your child will enjoy the book.
- Run your finger underneath the words as you read to signal that the print carries the story.
- Leave time for examining the illustrations more closely; encourage your child to find things in the pictures.
- Invite your youngster to join in whenever there's a repeated phrase in the text.
- Link up events in the book with similar events in your child's life.
- If your child asks a question, stop and answer it. The book can be a means to learning more about your child's thoughts.

Listening to Your Child Read Aloud

The support of your attention and praise is absolutely crucial to your child's continuing efforts to learn to read.

- If your child is learning to read and asks for a word, give it immediately so that the meaning of the story is not interrupted. DO NOT ask your child to sound out the word.
- On the other hand, if your child initiates the act of sounding out, don't intervene.
- If your child is reading along and makes what is called a miscue, listen for the sense of the miscue. If the word "road" is substituted for the word "street," for instance, no meaning is lost. Don't stop the reading for a correction.
- If the miscue makes no sense (for example, "horse" for "house"), ask your child to reread the sentence because you're not sure you understand what's just been read.
- Above all else, enjoy your child's growing command of print and make sure you give lots of praise. *You are your child's first teacher — and the most important one. Praise from you is critical for further risk-taking and learning.*

— Priscilla Lynch
Ph.D., New York University
Educational Consultant

To Shona and her new friends,
Arielle, Tamara, Rose, and Mike
—E. R. & D. B.

The artist and the editors would like
to thank Elaine Raphael for her creative help
in the painting of the illustrations.

Text copyright © 1997 by Margo Lundell.
Illustrations copyright © 1997 by Don Bolognese.
All rights reserved. Published by Scholastic Inc.
HELLO READER!, CARTWHEEL BOOKS, and the CARTWHEEL BOOKS logo
are registered trademarks of Scholastic Inc.

Library of Congress Cataloging-in-Publication Data

Lundell, Margo.
    Lad, a dog: best dog in the world / retold by Margo Lundell; based on
the book by Albert Payson Terhune; illustrated by Don Bolognese.
        p.   cm.—(Hello reader! Level 4)
    "Cartwheel books."
    Summary: Whisked from his country estate to compete in a dog
show in New York City, Lad is confused and unhappy and wishes only to
go home.
    ISBN 0-590-92974-7
    1. Dogs—Juvenile fiction. [1. Dogs—Fiction. 2. Dog shows—
Fiction. 3. New York (N.Y.)—Fiction.] I. Terhune, Albert Payson,
1872–1942. Lad, a dog. II. Bolognese, Don, ill. III. Title. IV. Series.
PZ10.3.L967Lad   1997
[Fic]—dc20   96-20937
                                                                  CIP
                                                                  AC

12 11 10 9 8 7 6 5 4 3 2   7 8 9/9 0 1 2/0

Printed in the U.S.A.   23

First Scholastic printing, April 1997

LAD, A DOG

Best Dog in the World

Retold by Margo Lundell

Based on the book by Albert Payson Terhune

Illustrated by Don Bolognese

Hello Reader! — Level 4

SCHOLASTIC INC.

New York   Toronto   London   Auckland   Sydney

L ad was a handsome, well-loved collie
who lived many years ago.
He came from a long line of champions.
He lived with his master and mistress
on a big country estate in New Jersey.

Every day Lad ran free
in the fields and forests.
He chased birds and squirrels.
He swam in a cool, clear lake.
Lad loved the Place with all his heart.

One winter a guest stayed at the Place.
The man thought Lad was the finest dog
he had ever seen.
"You should enter him in a show,"
the visitor told the master and mistress.

"There's a big dog show next month in New York City. I know Lad would win a blue ribbon."

"Maybe you're right," the mistress answered. "Lad *is* handsome. But he is more than that, too. He is noble and wise and good. A blue ribbon would honor him."

Soon the master was filling out the form
for the Westminster Dog Show.
But he entered Lad in only one class.
The class was called Novice.
It was for dogs that had never been
in a show before.

The master drove to the village with Lad.
They went to the post office
to mail the form.
"Good luck, Laddie," said the master.
Poor Lad did not know what lay ahead.
His life would soon change.

The master and mistress began to get
excited about the show.
They read everything about it
they could find.

The show was four days long.
Lad would have to stay at the show
for the whole four days.
The mistress began to worry.
"Lad will be lonely there at night,"
she said. "He has never been away
from home before."
Lad felt restless.
He sensed trouble in the air.

Then the show was only a week away.
Every day the mistress scrubbed Lad
in a hot bath.
Afterward she brushed him harder
than she ever had before.
Lad's beautiful coat began to shine.
It felt as soft as silk.

Lad looked wonderful.
But he felt miserable.
He was not allowed to run outdoors.
The strong soap smell hurt his nose.
The hard combing hurt his skin.
Why was this happening to him?

Then it was early on Wednesday morning.
It was time to drive into the city
for the first day of the dog show.
Lad watched his dear mistress climb
into the car.

"Come, Laddie!" she urged.
"Come, boy."
Lad didn't jump in the car as usual.
He didn't want to go for a ride that day.
"Hurry, Laddie!" said the master.
Finally the unhappy collie crawled
into the car.

As they drove off, Lad turned back
to look at the house.
He knew he was being taken away
from the place he loved.
His body sagged.
He was sick at heart.

The trip took less than two hours.
Then they were in the city.
The master parked the car.
He and the mistress hurried Lad
to the show.
Lad was in a daze.
The roar of the city was painful
to his ears.

The show was being held in a big arena
called Madison Square Garden.
The master and mistress brought Lad
to the entrance.
A dog doctor examined him quickly.
"Go ahead," said the vet. "He looks fine."
Lad could hear all the dogs barking
and howling in the arena ahead of them.
He stopped at the entrance
and looked up at the mistress sadly.
She touched his head with a loving hand.
"It's OK, Laddie," she whispered. "Come."
Lad started through the entrance.
He loved the master and mistress.
He would obey them no matter what.

The three of them stood in the huge
arena at last.
The noise was terrible.
Two thousand dogs were
entered in the show.
Hundreds of them were
barking at once.

The mistress held Lad's chain
and softly patted the confused dog.
Lad pressed against her for comfort.
The master went and found an attendant
to help them.
"Follow me, folks!" said the attendant.
"I'll show you where they put the collies."

The attendant led them past rows
and rows of open wire cages.
Great Danes barked at Lad.
Toy terriers yapped and snapped.
"Every dog is on a short chain," said
the mistress. "Lad isn't used to that."

Then they came to cage number 658.
"Up, Laddie!" said the mistress.
Lad slowly heaved himself up
into the cramped cell that would be
his home for the next few days.
The mistress fixed him some food,
but the unhappy dog would not eat.

Lad curled down in the straw.
The light was gone from his eyes.
Lad did not understand
why he was chained up.
The proud animal felt ashamed.
He thought he was being punished.

The master saw an old friend.
The man knew a lot about collies.
"Come and see our Lad," said the master,
pulling the man toward Lad's cage. "He's
not as nervous and skinny as these other
collies. Lad is all brains and heart."
"Brains and heart may not do him any
good here," said the collie man.

Lad paid no attention as the collie man
studied him.
"I'm sorry to say your dog has
the old-fashioned look," said the man.
"He's too big and wide for this year's style.
He should have smaller bones and be more
like a greyhound."

The mistress threw her arms around Lad. "I wouldn't change anything about him!" she cried. "I'm just sorry we came. I've never seen Lad so lifeless."

As the mistress spoke, Lad's Novice Class was called.

Unhappy Lad stayed close to the mistress
as they entered the show ring.
"Parade your dogs!" the judge called out.
The other Novice collies walked around
the ring with their trainers.

The others were thin, young show dogs
starting their careers.
The dogs wore choke collars that forced
them to hold their heads high.
Their fur was clipped in special ways.
Their ears had been trained to stand up.
The show dogs all looked fancier than Lad.

The judge was Scottish.
People said he was hard to please.
Mr. McGrath stopped the mistress
as she circled the ring with Lad.
"Please stand with your dog at the far
end," he said. "I want him out of the way
while I judge the others."

Slowly the mistress walked Lad
to a distant corner of the ring.
She wanted to cry.
Poor beautiful Lad.
She was sure he had been thrown out
of the Novice Class.
Lad sensed her sorrow.
He whined softly
and licked his dear mistress' hand.

One by one, the other collies stood
on the judge's platform.
The judge checked each dog well.
He looked at their teeth and their ears,
their shoulders and hips.
He didn't miss a thing.
Then the judge seemed to remember Lad.
He walked over and quickly ran his hands
through Lad's silky fur.
It was a short exam.
The mistress was sure Lad had lost.
"Shall I take him away now?" she asked
when Mr. McGrath was done.

The judge laid one hand on Lad's head.
In the other he held out a silk ribbon.
The ribbon was blue.
"Yes, you may go," said the judge.
"But take this with you."

The mistress had tears in her eyes.
She leaned down to clip the ribbon
to Lad's collar.
She kissed the top of his head quickly
so that no one would notice.
"Good Laddie!" she whispered
in the big dog's ear.

Mr. McGrath watched Lad leave the ring.
He was glad he had waved Lad aside
while he judged the other dogs.
With Lad nearby he might not have given
the others a fair exam.
The judge loved Lad's noble look.
He loved his deep chest and grand head.

Winning brought Lad no joy.
Soon he was back in his cell.
A new torment awaited him
because he had won a blue ribbon.
Collies who won their separate classes
were all expected to compete
in a Winners Class at the end of the day.

Hours later came the call for "Winners!"
For the second time Lad plodded
into the ring with the mistress.
Angus McGrath was the judge again.
But the mistress knew Lad had little
chance of winning.

This time he wasn't competing
against young newcomers.
This time he was up against
the best collies in the show.
The dog that took first place
would win a silver cup.

One by one, the dogs were weeded out.
Finally only two collies remained.
One was Lad.
The other was a grand champion
named Prince Carl.
The champion looked livelier and
much more eager than Lad.
The mistress wanted to help Lad.
She spoke to him in a low voice.
"We're going home, Laddie! Home!"
When Lad heard the word "home,"
his ears went up.
He looked alert and handsome.
Even so, Mr. McGrath turned toward
Prince Carl.

The judge laid his hand
on Prince Carl's head.
The mistress pulled Lad away.
"Wait!" snapped Mr. McGrath.
He was holding one of Prince Carl's
perfect ears.
He looked at it closely.
Thin bits of tape were holding
the dog's ears in position.
It was an old trick—and not legal.
Mr. McGrath stared at Prince Carl's trainer.
Then he put his hand on Lad's head.
"Your grand dog is the winner,"
he told the mistress.
The crowd cheered for Lad.

Suddenly Lad was a star.
Everyone reached out to pat him
after he left the ring.
The mistress did not take Lad
back to his hated cage.
She and the master went to find
one of the show's managers.

The mistress had a question
about the silver cup Lad had won.
"When will it be presented?" she asked.
"Not until Saturday night," the manager
answered. "And he must be there
to receive it."
The mistress looked at Lad.
She saw his sad eyes.

Tormenting Lad for three more days
would be too cruel.
The master and mistress agreed
that it was time to go.
"If you leave now, they won't let you
show the dog here again," said
the manager.
"I made Lad a promise," the mistress
replied. "And we're going home!"
The mistress turned to Lad.
"Home, boy, home!" she said.
Lad shivered with joy.
For the first time in the huge arena,
the giant collie began to bark.
His tail wagged.
His heart pounded.
Lad was going home.

— *About Lad* —

*The famous collie lived with the
talented animal and nature writer,
Albert Payson Terhune, and his wife
in Pompton Lakes, New Jersey. The
"Place" was a wooded estate called
Sunnybank.*

*A series of magazine stories about Lad
were published during World War I.
The stories were very popular. After the
war, the stories were published in a book.
The book about Lad sold very well.
The brave, loyal dog became so popular
that people would drive to Sunnybank
uninvited "to see where Lad lived."
The author was finally forced to put up
gates and keep them closed.*

*Terhune went on to write stories about
other dogs, but he was always best
known for the tales he told about the
collie. There was no other dog like Lad.
The author said it well in his dedication
to the book:*

This book is dedicated

to the memory of

LAD

thoroughbred in body and soul